TITOBI

A Love Story Rooted in Strength, Survival, and Divine Favor

Written by:

Invigorating Duchess

Graduate of the

School of Communications

Texas Southern University

Native of Louisiana

"Let your light so shine among men,

that they may see your good works

and glorify your Father which is in heaven."

— Matthew 5:16

Published by

Girl 14 Publishing

An Awthntkx Production Company

Chapter 1

The

Turmoil

Ann & Ivan

In the heart of the Tabasco capital of the world, just a few blocks from

the Konriko Rice Mill and around the corner from the historic Shadows-

on-the-Teche in New Iberia, Louisiana, a memorable event unfolded on

June 13, 1993. It was a Sunday morning that Titobi would never forget.

Perhaps the universe was still unsettled after Hurricane Andrew, as Titobi

was about to experience a day that felt like Friday the 13th.

On this day, Hulk Hogan defeated Yokozuna to become the World

Wrestling Federation Champion, and John Campbell passed away, leaving

for heaven. As the car horn honked in the driveway, it was Titobi's aunt,

signaling for her mother to hurry so they could attend the 11 AM service

at Cottrell Methodist Church. This church held deep family roots, with

Titobi's grandmother's name etched in the pews, detailing their family history.

As Titobi waved goodbye to her aunt and mother, who were on their way to church, she found herself alone, a rare occurrence. Titobi, a trust fund baby, had lost her father at the age of two, and her mother kept a close watch on her, knowing she was different and needed careful upbringing. Titobi's parents, her Louisiana-born mother and Texas-raised father, were known for their kindness, a trait Titobi inherited.

Shortly after her family left, the phone rang. It was Sheila, Titobi's third, cousin on her mother's side. Sheila, frustrated with an 18-year-old boy, sought advice from her 13-year-old cousin. Sheila had visited the boy the previous day, and he had run away, hurting her feelings. Sheila called

Titobi, who then called their cousins Marilyn and Wendy to discuss the situation and confront the boy.

Titobi, raised with her male cousins as if they were siblings, was tough and could fight very well. She had to be, growing up as a trust fund baby on Ann Street. When the boy disrespected Sheila, Titobi stood her ground, even giving him her address to come and fight. Titobi's male cousins had moved to Texas, and her mother was focused on raising her own children, but Titobi didn't need backup; she was fearless.

The boy arrived on a bicycle, ready to fight. Just as the confrontation was about to begin, Titobi's mother returned from church. The boy, who had recently graduated high school and managed the local Pizza Hut, turned into a saint in her presence. Titobi's mother, always seeking acceptance and recognition, saw an opportunity to connect with the

boy's large, well-known family. She named him Titobi's boyfriend,

ignoring the age gap and the fact that Titobi already had a boyfriend,

Tory, who was in California on a family vacation.

Craig, the boy, had no shame in pursuing a relationship with Titobi,

despite the age difference. He saw her bright spirit and attraction, but

Titobi, proud of her innocence, had no interest in him. She and her

friends considered him creepy, as he often talked about inappropriate

topics. Titobi spent much of her time at Wendy's house, avoiding Craig's

advances.

A little over six months after Titobi's mother forced her to break up with

Tory, things took a disturbing turn. Craig that 18-year-old with a reputation for being off-putting and strangely obsessive, began

showering Titobi with gifts: jewelry, compliments, attention. All the

gestures of romantic interest that might seem appropriate...if Titobi

weren't just thirteen. The adults around her looked the other way,

blinded by superficial charm or distracted by their own chaos.

Titobi had always drawn attention in her neighborhood. With whispers of

a wealthy grandmother in Texas and a trust fund waiting in the wings,

she was envied, resented, and deeply misunderstood. Her brilliance only

added to the hostility. The maternal side of her family never embraced

her, and the community never forgave her for the privileges they

assumed she had. The root of their hatred was money—but the wound

went far deeper.

Then came Brad. He was new to the neighborhood—fresh from Uptown, where the housing projects painted a different story than the downtrodden blocks Downtown. Brad's rough demeanor clashed instantly with Titobi's grace. She found him loud, aggressive, and unappealing—not because she felt superior, but because he simply wasn't her type. Brad misread her rejection as arrogance, and that resentment simmered until it curdled into something violent.

Karen—the neighborhood bully and self-appointed gossip queen—connected with Brad through his sister. Together, they plotted against Titobi. Karen had been watching her for years, picking at her spirit from the corner stoops and whispered circles. She knew Titobi's routines. She knew her mother's nightly ritual: bingo at 7 p.m., like clockwork.

And she knew about Craig-how he'd started dropping by after the

mother left, hanging out with Titobi and her friend Wendy as if that

were normal. In Craig's mind, it was. Some said Craig had been

victimized as a child, perhaps molested by one of his older brothers.

Whatever his past, he carried darkness-and zero respect for a child's

right to safety.

One night, Karen gave Brad the go-ahead. She told him exactly when

Titobi would be alone. Brad waited until her mother left for bingo. Titobi,

thinking Craig had circled back, opened the door.

Instead, Brad shoved her inside.

He threw her onto the couch, muffling her cries. Her uncle-diagnosed

with schizophrenia-was in the back room, disconnected from reality. Brad pulled at her clothes, assaulting her. But Titobi fought back. She reached

for a heavy glass ashtray on the coffee table and struck him in the head.

He fled.

In a daze, she called 911. Craig showed up moments later—too late to

intervene, but early enough to view her suffering as a theft. He'd seen

her body as something he had a twisted claim to, and now that someone

else had assaulted her, he became obsessed. Possessive. His behavior

grew more aggressive, more disturbing.

Craig began threatening her. Coercing her. Manipulating her innocence.

He would ask her about her menstrual cycle, track her ovulation like a

predator with a plan. What 13-year-old understands that kind of

danger? He wanted to get her pregnant. Wanted to be a father like his older siblings. Everyone in his family welcomed Titobi like she was one of their own—no one seemed to care that she was still a child.

When Titobi turned 14, Craig made his move. Again, her mother left for bingo. Again, there was no one to stop him. Months of psychological torment had laid the groundwork. He forced her into acts she didn't understand, threatening to lie to her mother, telling her that if she didn't comply, he'd ruin her image as a "good girl."

The irony was cruel: when Titobi was first taken to the hospital after Brad's assault, her mother's concern wasn't just the trauma—it was whether Titobi had ever had sex before. Titobi, trying desperately to hold onto her mother's approval, had insisted she hadn't. Craig used that desperation against her. He twisted her truth, her vulnerability, into a

weapon.

With her father deceased, her protective male relatives miles away in

Texas, and her mentally ill uncle incapable of defending her, Titobi stood

alone against a cycle of abuse no one around her was willing to

interrupt.

And so, on November 5th, 1994, at the age of fourteen, Titobi gave birth

to an 8 lb. 7 oz. baby girl. She brought life into the world—and bore the

weight of a trauma that had its roots in silence, shame, and generational

negligence. A wound so deep it echoed like a scripture. Like prophecy.

Chapter 1.5

The Weight

of

Two

Daughters

After surviving an unbearable teenage life in New Iberia, Titobi moved to Galveston, Texas-carrying with her not just two daughters, but a mountain of pain. Craig had violated her not once but twice, then humiliated her by marrying another woman. He left her pregnant and alone, telling her she was "less than" because she couldn't give him a son.

Both women-Titobi and Craig's new bride-carried Craig's children at the same time. Titobi gave birth to her second daughter on December 17, 1995. Craig's son, Craig Jr., was born just two months and ten days later, on February 7, 1996. Craig turned his son into a weapon-lording him over Titobi as proof of her supposed failure. He had one of the biggest weddings New Iberia had ever seen, shotgun-style, just before Craig Jr.

arrived. The message was clear: Titobi, with her daughters, was disposable.

In Galveston, Titobi met Daryl-a different breed of tormentor. A washed-up high school football star who never made it past his college dreams. His confidence was inflated, but his spirit was rotten. Titobi, with only a 7th-grade education at the time, became the target of his cruelty. In his eyes, she was just another teenage mother with a failed past.

She had already endured so much beaten, raped, robbed, bullied. New Iberia had never shown her mercy. Even before birth, she was marked, rumored to be a "trust fund baby" because of her father's on-the-job injury after her conception. The whispers painted her as rich and privileged-a target before she could even walk.

Galveston gave her breathing room, but not freedom. The shadows of New Iberia followed people with ties to her father spread rumors, and the secret of her trust fund stalked her dreams. She tried to disappear into the background. Tried to live quietly. But pain has a way of finding those who carry light.

Daryl—son of an adulterer and a woman scorned by the streets—had no idea he'd been blessed with Titobi. And he never treated her like a gift. Embarrassed by her weight, her lack of education, and her vulnerability, he secretly married her, refusing to claim her publicly. The first four years of their marriage were a private hell.

They had a son—not out of love, but to seal the cracks in their unraveling union. A child meant to prove something to Craig and the folks back in

New Iberia. A false display of happiness to cloak the misery beneath.

Daryl went AWOL from the military, and the couple returned to New

Iberia under the guise of homecoming. But Daryl had never been a

soldier. Not for Titobi. Not for his country. Not even for his own

children.

By 2005, Titobi—now a mother of three and finally enrolled at UL

Lafayette pursuing journalism—made the decision to leave. She'd survived

a suicide attempt. She had fought through years of mental abuse. But

Daryl wasn't ready to release his grip. He tested her boundaries nightly,

removing and replacing her rings while she slept—to measure how deeply

she slept. That's how he kept control.

Only God knows how many times Daryl assaulted her while she slept.

But the final time was unforgettable. She had told him she was leaving.

And she woke up to Daryl in full sweat, having sexually violated her once

again impregnating her with a child she never consented to create.

She felt no love for Daryl, romantically or spiritually. Her heart had been

long tangled with Gabriel and Tony, not the man who treated her like less

than a dog. They were already surviving the trauma of Hurricane Katrina,

displaced and broken. At just 26 weeks, Titobi gave birth to her second

son—a miracle born of misery.

She named him Messiah.

Because from conception to delivery, there was no explanation but God.

Somehow, she had survived Daryl's abuse-and the cruelty of his family, too. His cousin GiGi was especially vicious, convinced that Titobi believed herself superior. But the truth was simpler.

Like Karen before her, GiGi saw the spiritual light in Titobi's soul. Some people-those consumed by darkness-are bound to hate what shines.

Titobi had spent years learning that lesson the hard way.

Now she sat in the quiet sanctuary of her mega church in Houston, tucked away in the prayer room where the city's noise could not touch her. The room was warm with candlelight, soft gospel spilling from a nearby speaker, and the scent of frankincense clinging to her thoughts like memory.

Her mind drifted.

. Her days were packed with effort-mothering five children, navigating healing, pursuing dreams-and her nights were haunted by echoes that refused to fade. The rapes. The betrayals. The lies that shaped her childhood. The weddings she was never invited to. The children born from abuse, and the shame that was never hers to carry-but was placed upon her anyway.

She closed her eyes and remembered pain and betrayal.She remembered Craig's cruelty; his absence dressed as triumph. She remembered Daryl's manipulation, his theft of her body while she slept, his cowardice hidden behind fake pride and heavy hands. And she remembered naming her second son Messiah-not from hope in Daryl, but from faith in God.

Because the birth of her last son with Daryl, after so much abuse, could

only mean one thing:

She had survived.

Every candle around her flickered as if in agreement. Every tear that

refused to fall held the weight of generations. Her life was stained by

the abuse of men, the silence of women, and the envy of those who

couldn't stand how brightly she glowed.

But Titobi was still glowing.

Her days were filled with challenges, and her nights were haunted by

the echoes of her past. Turmoil seemed to be her constant companion,

and peace was a distant dream.

Titobi's life was a tapestry of struggles. She faced betrayal from those she trusted, endured hardships that tested her spirit, and navigated a world that often seemed indifferent to her pain. Yet, through it all, she held onto a flicker of hope, a small but persistent belief that there was something greater waiting for her.

As she knelt in prayer, tears streaming down her face, Titobi poured out her heart. She spoke of her fears, her doubts, and her longing for solace. In that moment, she felt a presence, a comforting embrace that seemed to whisper words of reassurance. It was as if God Himself was listening, offering her the strength she so desperately needed.

Chapter 2

The

Betrayal

Titobi's life had always been a series of ups and downs, but the betrayal she faced was unlike anything she had ever experienced. It came from those she trusted the most, those she considered family. The pain was sharp and deep, leaving her feeling isolated and vulnerable.

She had always been a pillar of strength for her friends, offering support and guidance whenever they needed it. But when she needed them the most, they turned their backs on her. The betrayal was a harsh reminder of the fragility of human relationships and the unpredictability of life.

The betrayal began subtly, with whispers and rumors that spread like wildfire. Titobi noticed the change in her friends' behavior, the way they avoided her gaze and spoke in hushed tones when she was around. She tried to confront them, but they denied any wrongdoing, leaving her feeling confused and paranoid.

As the days passed, the situation escalated. Titobi discovered that her friends had been conspiring against her, spreading false accusations and tarnishing her reputation. They had manipulated others to believe their lies, turning the community she once cherished into a hostile environment. The betrayal was not just a personal attack; it was a calculated effort to destroy her sense of belonging and trust.

Titobi's heart was heavy with sorrow, and her mind was clouded with confusion. She questioned everything she had ever believed in, wondering if there was any truth or loyalty left in the world. The turmoil in her life seemed to intensify, and she struggled to find a way out of the darkness.

Despite the pain, Titobi refused to give up. She knew that she had to find a way to heal and move forward. She sought solace in the quiet moments, reflecting on her past and searching for answers. It was during these moments that she remembered scripture and god's promises to his children.

Chapter 2.5

The

Ultimate

Betrayal

2016 arrived with spring air that felt strangely fresh, like false hope.

A therapist had once suggested that Titobi's oldest daughter showed signs of a deep spiritual darkness, symptoms that couldn't be explained by the environment alone. The therapist also noted a troubling pattern—mental illness in Craig's bloodline, tied to his maternal grandparents who were allegedly first cousins. It was a painful possibility Titobi couldn't ignore.

She'd spent years shielding her daughter from Craig's influence. But now, desperate for answers, she reached out to him—hoping he'd show up as a father, even briefly.

Craig saw a door opening.

And like the opportunist he'd always been, he slipped in with his usual

intentions: not to help, but to harm. He had never stopped hating Titobi.

Not even after all these years. Not even now that she was a graduate

student, ranked in the top 7% nationwide on her LSAT. Her success only

made his hatred sharper.

Craig wasn't alone in his vendetta. Somehow, he aligned with Daryl—

another enemy cloaked in family ties. Together, they waged a spiritual

and legal war against her. They weaponized their partners, finances, and

even black magic. Nothing was off-limits in their pursuit of her

destruction.

This wasn't a new terrain for Titobi. She had lived in and out of

courtrooms since her teenage years, always fighting to prove herself as a worthy mother, always battling false charges, CPS investigations, and

whispered attacks. Craig's sister worked in law enforcement. His

extended family was embedded in the legal system. They leveraged

those connections mercilessly, dragging her into courtroom after

courtroom, trying to bury her beneath bureaucracy and lies.

And still, she held her ground.

What she didn't realize was that Craig and Daryl weren't just after her

they had set sights on her children. Titobi's oldest daughter had always

been complicated, carrying an envy that festered quietly. It was this envy

that Craig and Daryl manipulated, turning her daughter into a weapon.

Titobi watched in disbelief as her four oldest children began pulling away-confused, angry, caught in a web spun by men who should never have been near them to begin with.

Her daughter's betrayal was the deepest wound yet.

It wasn't just a rebellion. It was spiritual sabotage. A mother's greatest nightmare.

They used her own children to beat her down-emotionally, legally, and spiritually.

And still, Titobi stood.

Chapter 3

A Psalm

and a

Silence

Before Titobi ever spoke in tongues, she forgot how to speak altogether.

It was the winter of 1995. Craig had just humiliated her-abandoning her

with a second baby on the way while marrying another woman, parading

their wedding through New Iberia with shotgun fanfare. Her voice didn't

break-it vanished. The emotional trauma rendered her non-verbal.

People assumed she was withdrawn. But what she was feeling couldn't

be voiced.

She was carrying another daughter. Craig had demanded a son, and her

failure to produce one became another excuse for him to disappear. She

felt like a walking sin.

Her mother, not a preacher but always spiritually tuned in, noticed the

silence growing heavier. One night she walked into the bedroom and placed a Bible in Titobi's hands-opened to Psalm 23. Titobi traced the

words with her finger:

"The Lord is my shepherd; I shall not want..."

She couldn't read them aloud. But she could feel them. And that became

the beginning of her journey with God.

It wasn't sudden redemption. It was survival. That scripture became her

anchor as she learned to communicate through prayer, through

journaling, through divine stillness. God saw the voice trapped inside

her-and waited patiently while it rebuilt.

The trauma continued. Craig didn't stop. He had proposed to her, with

her cousin accepting the ring, just to force himself deeper into her

family. Desperate to play house with a 14-year-old, he even secured a rental home-pressuring her into an adult life when she still longed for

childhood. He didn't love her. He wanted to control her.

So much of her girlhood was swallowed by obligation and manipulation.

School didn't feel safe either, not regular school, at least.

Titobi was enrolled in the city's pregnancy program-she sat every day

between Tina and Miley, girls just like her, who had learned to fight

before they ever learned to dream. Tina was on her third child at just 14.

Miley was carrying her second. Uptown girls, hardened by generational

war.

One day in class, Miley pulled out a hammerhead wrapped in a sock. A

weapon. For protection against her baby daddy's other girlfriend, another teenager, also pregnant, sitting just rows away. That was the classroom

dynamic. The building pulsed with rage and fear.

In that chaos, Tony arrived.

Chapter 3.5

Green Skirts

and

Psalms

Tony was 6'7". Regal. creole. Uptown through and through. He looked

like a model and moved like a man with morals. He caught Titobi's eye

instantly—but never made a move.

Not because he didn't want to.

But because he saw the danger.

He told Marvin, her close friend, "I see the guy who drops her off. I don't

want no drama." He was talking about Craig—the possessive older

boyfriend who treated Titobi like a wife and a prisoner. Craig circled the

school like he owned it, staring down anyone who had looked at her too

long.

Tony kept his distance. But he saw her.

Not just her weight, which had ballooned past 400 pounds under stress and grief.

He saw her beauty. Her light. Her mind.

He encouraged her to keep herself up-to wear colors that made her glow, to stay polished even in pain. "You're more than what they say you are," he once told her. "Don't let the mirror lie to you."

Those words stayed.

And then, on December 24, 1996, they crossed paths again.

🕊

Titobi was wearing a green mini skirt that hugged her curves and showed off her honey-brown legs. She had styled herself with intention, not for anyone else-but for herself.

Tony spotted her across the street and approached with a smile.

"Hey-I remember you. You were at the pregnancy school, right?"

Titobi lit up. "I remember you too. You're the finest man God ever created."

Seventeen, both a little older now, both knowing the world had already tried to break them, they laughed like kids. That moment became the start of a bond that would stretch across decades.

Through marriages. Babies. Silence and celebration.

Tony was her consistent reminder that love didn't have to hurt. He never tried to control her. Never wanted anything from her but truth.

Until 2023.

New Iberia resurfaced on social media—the same shadows and gossip, rebranded for a digital age. Tony, under pressure, publicly distanced himself from her. The betrayal hit hard. Titobi had never expected romance. But she had always counted on realness. Tony was the one person who never changed up.

Now he had.

And that moment made her realize it was time to stop romanticizing the white picket fence. Tony wasn't the dream anymore. He had become part of the disappointment.

But not the death of her hope.

She still wore green sometimes. She still reads Psalm 23. She still kept

her hair and nails together-even when it hurt to stand in the mirror.

Because her voice had returned.

And now, she used it without apology.

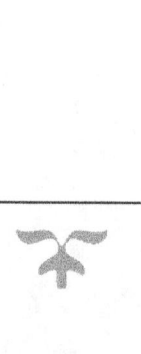

Chapter 4

Love That

Felt

Like Rescue

In 2005, Titobi met Gabriel—a tall, magnetic Creole man from a small place called Loreauville, just outside New Iberia. He was 6'6", smooth-skinned and striking, with deep-set eyes that seemed to carry both wisdom and warning. Gabriel had the look of a movie star and the soul of a boy raised by old-school elders. His grandmother and grandfather had kept him close, trying to protect him from the life waiting on the corners.

He was street-undeniably. Raised in a crime-connected family that ran deep through Iberia Parish. But Gabriel was fighting—against addiction, abandonment, and generational curses. He wasn't free, but he was trying. And that fight made him relatable.

Titobi met Gabriel at UL Lafayette. She was attending college out of

family obligation, chasing purpose even when the path felt borrowed.

Gabriel wasn't a student in spirit-he was there for other reasons, floating

through campus in his own rhythm. But their paths crossed. And when

they did, Gabriel saw something in her.

Not pity. Not possession.

Worth.

He took her on dates, simple and sweet. He opened the doors. Paid

attention. Brought her home to his grandmother's house, introduced her

as someone precious. He called her "baby girl" like it meant something

eternal. And he reminded her-again and again-that she was worthy of

gentleness, of devotion.

It was different from Tony.

Tony had been her consistent comfort, her mirror. But Gabriel brought

fire. He poured into her like a man who understood what it meant to

love without rules, because he'd lived a life where rules always came

with consequences.

For once, Titobi didn't feel like a problem needing to be fixed. She felt

like a woman worth showing off.

But the shadows always waited.

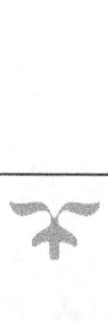

When the

News Broke

She didn't see it coming. Not fully.

Gabriel had demons, and they weren't small. He moved in circles that blurred morality. Drugs. Hustle. Affiliations that didn't align with the woman Titobi was becoming.

And then one evening, while she was folding laundry and her youngest was babbling in the living room, she heard the anchor say his name.

Evening news.

Drug trafficking charges.

A federal sting that had been months in motion.

They showed his photo-her Gabriel. The man who kissed her hand after

dinner. The man who told her she had purpose. He was in handcuffs, led

into a courthouse in silence, his head down and expression blank.

Her body went cold.

This wasn't Tony disappearing into the silence. This was Gabriel

detonating in plain sight.

She remembered their walks. Their laughter. Their intimate talks about

childhood pain and future hope. She remembered how he said, "I ain't

perfect, but I swear I'm trying for you." And she believed him.

But this...this was something she couldn't outrun.

She had children watching. Papers due. A whole degree to finish. And a

calling that didn't include compromise. Gabriel wasn't evil. But he was

unstable. And she was done sacrificing her peace for potential.

So, she let go.

Not bitterly. But firmly.

Because if the 23rd Psalm taught her anything, it was that restoration

required discipline—and sometimes distance.

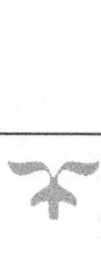

Chapter 5

Walk That

Walk, Sis

Texas Southern didn't just educate Titobi. It healed her.

She moved to Houston in the aftermath of Hurricane Katrina storm that scattered lives like paper in the wind. By 2011, she'd transferred out of ULL and into the legendary halls of Texas Southern University. August 25th, 2011, would become a turning point. Unbeknownst to her, it was the eve of her first and second strokes, brought on by exhaustion, trauma, and the constant need to outrun Daryl's threats. She was working two jobs and chasing a degree while dodging danger-and her body couldn't keep up.

But her spirit didn't break.

Texas Southern wrapped her in arms wide as the skyline.

Enrolling in the School of Communications, Titobi flourished. In 2012-

2013, she was crowned Ms. Entertainment Management-a title that felt

less like recognition and more like prophecy. She was no longer just

surviving. She was thriving. Living. Laughing. Dreaming.

Her classes were often taught by Mathew Knowles, the architect behind

Destiny's Child. His presence was more than inspirational-he saw her.

They talked about New Iberia over plates of her home-cooked meals. He

encouraged Titobi and her classmates to seek ownership, not just

opportunity. Especially as Black creatives in a business built to exploit

their gifts.

"Don't wait on corporate America to validate you," he told her once.

"Build it. Brand it. Own it."

And she did.

She opened her first comedy showcase at TSU, hosting for the now-deceased comic legend Tyler Craig-whose sharp wit and gritty truth-telling mirrored her own journey. The laughter that night was different. It was healing.

Texas Southern has birthed greatness for generations. With historic alumni like Congresswoman Barbara Jordan, Michael Strahan, Mickey Leland, and Megan Thee Stallion, TSU is more than an HBCU-it's a sacred ground for Black excellence, advocacy, and unapologetic ambition. It holds space in American history as a university where protest met policy and where cultural movements took root. For Titobi, it was the first place she saw what being part of a Black family really felt like-loving, layered, messy, meaningful.

Her heart belonged to the Ocean of Soul, TSU's legendary marching band. She followed them everywhere, crying tears she didn't have words for each time they passed by in uniform. There was something about the rhythm-the roar of brass and bass-that reminded her she had survived something unspeakable and still kept time with destiny.

During her time at TSU, she built the blueprint for her future. She started multiple businesses. She met lifelong friend Wilson Johnson, a connector of hearts and communities. He exposed her to family and legacy beyond biology, giving her emotional scaffolding she'd been missing.

And even now, when the world feels heavy, Titobi drives to campus and sits, just to pray. Just to feel the echo of drums and hope. Just to remember who she is when the world tries to forget.

TSU taught her not just to walk—it taught her to walk with power. With pride. With purpose.

To walk that walk, sis.

Chapter 5.5

Welcome

to

Houston

Titobi

Texas Southern University wasn't just a campus—it was redemption in brick and soul.

For the first time, Titobi felt what it was like to live boldly, without apology. She was on her dream campus, studying Communications, surrounded by people who didn't know her history, her battles, or the whispers of trust fund rumors. And that was the gift—she could just be herself. No masks. No explanations.

Her classes gave her life. The Ocean of Soul band stirred her spirit. Her friend group accepted her fully. She was finally experiencing what she called a "normal life"—the kind of student experience she'd once believed was reserved for someone else.

And then, Brittany happened.

One day in class, Titobi shared details about a weekend trip to Louisiana

and a date with a man named Marcus. Brittany rolled her eyes with love.

"Girl, why are you still messing with Louisiana men?" She had a point.

"You're in Houston now. You need a Houston experience. Real city love. I

got you."

Without waiting for permission, Brittany created an online dating profile

for her. Requirements? Must be born and raised in Houston. Street-

smart, attractive, and-above all-interesting.

Later that day, she passed Titobi a note in class:

"Blind date. 7PM. Be cute."

The guy? Buttery brown skin. Light brown eyes. Half Black, half Indian. Articulate like a poet. Self-taught tech wizard who built PCs from scratch. No formal education—but vocabulary rich enough to rival T.I.

The date was a mix of magic and confusion. He showed up with luggage in his car, clearly homeless and searching for shelter. Titobi, not new to red flags, lied about her address and made a mental note: This is a no.

Still, he was a Scorpio. Sexual, unpredictable, impulsive. And Titobi—fresh out of trauma and stepping into her divine femininity—wasn't turning down a good time. Their physical chemistry was undeniable. It reminded her of Tony One—fiery, passionate, complicated.

But Tony Two was twelve years younger, emotionally erratic, and–

unbeknownst to her–carrying the weight of multiple baby mamas. Not

two. Not three. More like twenty-five.

And she was about to become one of them.

She didn't even know she was pregnant that night she beat his a**–she

just knew Tony had her messed up.

The memory plays in her mind like a movie. And honestly, it's still

funny–especially when her cousin Cody retells it. Cody, who was just

three years older, raised her like a little sister and trained her like a

soldier. He taught her to fight as a kid so she could always hold her own,

especially against boys. Whether God sees that as a blessing or a flaw,

one thing's for sure–Titobi was never soft.

And when grown men tried her? She could call Cody. He had gang ties

and real backup. But with Tony the Second?

She didn't need help. She had this one.

Tony was light work. Maybe 5'7", 145 lbs. soaking wet. Titobi had been

knocking out grown men since fifth grade-Tony wasn't even a warm-up.

The altercation started one Saturday night. Tony barged into her room,

ranting about some social media foolishness. Titobi paid him no mind.

She wasn't moved by drama-never had been. As a child dragged through

custody battles, trust fund disputes, and court chaos between her mother,

grandmother, and Baby Daddy #1, she'd learned that chaos didn't deserve

her energy.

So, she stayed calm, reading her Bible in peace, until Tony made his

mistake.

He snatched the Bible from her hands and threw it to the floor.

Now he had her attention.

She stood up without saying a word. Slipped into her old Madea house

dress and laced up her *"fighting Jordans"-*the pair she kept in the

closet strictly for moments like this.

She stepped into the living room. Tony was still loud mouthing about

how he was going to knock her out.

Cody, living with her at the time, was laughing-on the toilet. He knew

exactly what was coming. After all, he'd trained her. He'd seen her in

action.

Tony walked into the bathroom while Cody was mid-number two, still

hurling threats like they were punches. "Man, get your cousin before I

knock her out!" he shouted. Cody, grinning, said something like, "You

better fight back instead of talking'."

Tony didn't listen.

Titobi had had enough.

She waited until he came back into the living room, then sucker-punched

him dead in the center of his face.

He kept talking.

She kept punching.

Two, three, four, five... six, seven, eight.

Tony ran to the kitchen, rummaging through drawers, clearly looking for a knife. When he found one, he paused-realizing he might be in over his head. So, he put it back and sprinted toward the back door. But Titobi beat him there.

She planted herself like a wall, and as he tried to reach the handle- boom-another one-two combo to the face.

Tony kept screaming for Cody. But Cody just came out of the bathroom, smirking, telling him to "defend himself like a real 713 Texas baby." Titobi was still swinging.

Tony ran to the garage, hit the button, and tried to escape. He was small and fast-but Titobi, a full 400 pounds of pure power, rolled under the garage door before it could close, landed on her feet like a pro boxer-and gave him at least a dozen more punches before he took off into the street.

He ran several blocks before collapsing in a neighbor's yard. Told them a gang had jumped him. Call 911. Sent police on a wild goose chase.

All because he was too scared to admit...

He got beat down by a woman.

Chapter 5.75

Tribe of One

It all started with fifty pregnancy tests.

Not for her-but for her daughter.

Titobi suspected her oldest child was pregnant after her younger

daughter mentioned missed periods. So, she did what only she would do:

bought fifty tests, planted herself at the front door, and waited.

But as she sat there, she had a thought:

When was the last time I had my own cycle?

She took a test. Then another. Then ten.

And then the truth:

She was pregnant. Again.

Baby number five. Her third son.

With the most chaotic man she'd ever entertained.

She had assumed she was baby mama number three. Turns out, she was baby mama number five...in a lineup of more than two dozen. Tony Two had fathered children across the country-he had recently fled Tennessee after impregnating another woman. That child was still an infant.

He had twin daughters in Houston-his pride and joy, not because they were the most gifted or well-behaved, but because in the hood, twins meant pride-a badge of honor in a broken system.

But Titobi wasn't competing.

She prayed.

Asked God for insight. For a name. For spiritual guidance.

And the answer came: Ezekiel.

She read the Book of Ezekiel through tears and exhaustion. Hospitalized for 29 days. Delivered via C-section, surrounded by 29 medical professionals. And when she called the father to share the birth, he insulted her recovery, calling her lazy for having a medically needed C-section.

He wasn't there. He couldn't be. He was in jail-for attempting to kill the woman in Dallas Another woman. Another child.

His pattern was shame. Hers was survival.

So, she named her son Ezekiel.

And moved forward. Again.

Alone. But alive.

Hurt. But whole.

Because once again, she survived the man who tried to leave her for

dead.

🕊

Chapter 6

Mirror, Mirror

The love affair wasn't with a man-it was with herself.

After years of being overlooked, overworked, and almost destroyed, Titobi finally saw herself clearly. Not just the pain or the trauma. She saw the brilliance. The beauty. The purpose. And she fell in love so deeply with her reflection that people started calling her conceited.

Maybe she was.

But when you've clawed your way out of spiritual abandonment, emotional betrayal, and generational neglect, loving yourself loudly is a revolution. She walked into rooms like she had equity in every conversation. Her skin glowed. Her hair gave statement. Her wardrobe sang. Her nails spoke legacy, and her smile? Her smile was proof of survival.

Her fashion embodied resilience. Her laughter carried testimony. She

didn't wait for compliments—she mirrored them. And when people asked

who she was dating, she replied, "My future."

She was building empires: podcasts, book drafts, branding concepts,

community advocacy. She didn't need a co-star. She was the whole cast.

And for a while, that love held her upright—until the world cracked again.

Jackpot!!!

TITOBI had hit the jackpot—everything she wanted, needed, dreamed of

was at Texas Southern. It was all there. The people, the energy, the

rhythm. She met so many who would forever be part of her story: from

Marquees to Jamarque.

And then there was Kirkland.

Kirkland wasn't a student at Texas Southern University-Kirkland was a gym. A Third Ward landmark. But Kirkland the man? Half Asian, half Black, fine as ever, with a political mind that could slice through fog. His worldview was sharp, layered, and deeply rooted.

Through her Third Ward ties and Mr. Johnson's connections, TITOBI met Quentin.

Quentin wasn't formally educated at TSU, but he was a pillar in her pursuit of an entertainment career. A gift waiting to happen. He was the salt in her pot of soup-bringing flavor, grounding, and exactly what she needed on the production side, especially as she built with Awthntkx Productions.

At Texas Southern, most of her professors were in the industry-the

Hollywood industry.

The most unforgettable? Mr. Mathew Knowles.

Once Titobi and Mathew began exchanging dialogue, something clicked.

He knew her hometown-New Iberia, Louisiana-and that familiarity

bonded them instantly. He was honest. Straight up. Despite being a

billionaire, he carried a sense of homeliness that stuck to Titobi like glue.

I mean seriously-this was the man who curated the group she watched

on TV and idolized.

And every single time she sat across from Mathew Knowles at brunch, it

felt like God had cracked open a little piece of heaven and let her walk

in.

She didn't brag.

She didn't post.

She didn't even tell her mama.

Because in New Iberia, sacred things had to be protected.

Her mother-known as the porch gossiper of the town, would've

considered it bragging. And bragging in New Iberia could get you killed.

In New Iberia, you didn't speak on your accomplishments unless the

community gave you a pass.

You had to be deemed "worthy" of celebration.

And Titobi? She learned the hard way-New Iberia would never clap for

her.

Not if she was Beyoncé's personal chef.

Not if she was flying first class around the globe.

Not if she built an empire from scratch.

New Iberia would always see her as "showing off."

Trying to be more than.

Trying to be seen.

And they would never recognize her.

It took her years to accept that truth.

But at Texas Southern, with the relationships she built—and with Mr.

Johnson, her lifelong friend—Titobi found something different.

She knew now:

New Iberia would always be behind her.

A place of memories, yes.

But never a place where she could live out her full potential.

Never a place where she could be who God created her to be.

Titobi always understood that in order to be successful, she had to

release every tie to New Iberia—including her own mother.

While she was at Texas Southern University, she went two full years

without speaking to her.

Because survival meant sacrifice.

Because earning her degree meant choosing herself—even if it meant

ostracizing the woman who gave her life.

And when graduation day came, no one showed up.

Not her family.

Not a soul from New Iberia.

Darrell, Craig, Tony—they should've been proud.

She had given birth to their offspring.

They should've been front row, clapping, shouting, claiming her.

But Titobi knew better.

She would never get cheers from men who preyed on her downfall and

prayed for her demise.

So she walked that stage alone.

And when her name was called, there was no roar.

No applause.

Maybe three or four claps from classmates.

But Mr. Johnson?

Front and center.

Camera in hand.

Already there before she arrived.

He took the pictures.

He got the video.

He was proud of her-period.

Titobi never needed much when it came to acceptance.

She grew up with so much hatred from her biological family, she didn't

expect love to come easy.

But to have one person in her corner-one person who believed she could

conquer the world and pushed her to do it-that meant everything.

You don't need a crowd.

You need a witness.

And if God sends you one person who sees you, affirms you, and walks with you?

That's a blessing.

That's divine alignment.

Titobi feels like she received the greatest blessing God could ever give her–having Mr. Johnson by her side.

Of all the things she took from Texas Southern University–her degree, her time with Mathew Knowles, the Ocean of Soul, the band, the friendships–Mr. Johnson was the true gift.

She met so many people who poured into her.

There was her peer counselor, a woman so stunning she could've graced the cover of any magazine. She resembled Nicole Ari Parker–half

Caucasian, half African American—and she was firmly in Titobi's corner.

Always encouraging her:

"Reach for the stars.

Pull them down.

Ride on them."

Titobi never imagined she'd find all of this at Texas Southern.

Support.

Affirmation.

Legacy.

But even after carrying her mother's body at the funeral, even after

showing her what real friendship looked like, what real love felt like,

what a real man could be—Mr. Johnson remained the constant.

The one who showed up.

The one who stood tall.

The one who supported her in ways she didn't even know were possible.

Her greatest takeaway wasn't just the degree.

It was the presence of someone who loved her without condition.

And that will always be Mr. Johnson.

Chapter 7

The Bat

&

The Burial

January 2020 changed everything.

It wasn't a slow descent. It was a sudden silence.

Her mother walked into the emergency room, laid on the table-and died.

No known illness. No previous sickness. Just a quiet surrender that stunned everyone. Titobi lost her greatest protector, her spiritual compass, her truth teller. The woman who handed her Psalm 23 and watched her rise in silence had now returned to God without warning.

And Titobi was shattered.It was absolutely devastating how Titobi lost her mother.

At 2:00 PM, they were on the phone.

Her mother was reassuring her, saying everything would be okay.

By 5:00 PM, her baby brother was knocking on the door to tell her their

mother had died.

No warning.

No preparation.

No time to brace for impact.

People don't realize how blessed they are when their parents pass from

illnesses like Alzheimer's or cancer—those slow, painful diseases that at

least give you time to prepare, to say goodbye.

Titobi had none of that.

Her mother had just moved to Houston.

They had only recently rekindled their once-damaged, broken

relationship.

Two weeks.

Just two weeks of healing, laughter, and hope.

They were finally in a beautiful place as mother and daughter.

Titobi felt like she could finally live life and enjoy her mother.

But that joy was short-lived.

Their relationship had been deeply affected by trauma—by the sexual

assault from Craig, by Titobi becoming a teenage mother, by the years

she felt unprotected and unheard.

It had been a painful, complicated bond.

And just when they had found common ground, just when they were

finally on the same page—her mother was gone.

That kind of loss doesn't just break your heart.

It rewrites it.

Isn't that God?

Isn't that what we're all here to do—live out our purpose, and when that

purpose is fulfilled, return home to our Heavenly Father?

Titobi and her mother had finally made amends.

Finally loving each other like mother and daughter.

Finally healing what had been broken for years.

And in that divine moment, her mother's purpose was complete.

The order had been set.

She could go home—to be with her own mother, her sisters, her people.

Titobi's mother had been the last of six children still living.

No mother. No father. No siblings.

She often spoke of death—not with fear, but with longing.

She dreamed of reunion.

She dreamed of peace.

She dreamed of Heaven.

And that was the comfort Titobi held in her heart:

Her mother was exactly where she wanted to be.

With God.

With her people.

Finally whole.

But don't think for one second that New Iberia gave Titobi space to

mourn.

Not a breath. Not a moment. Not a sliver of grace.

Her third Cousin Letitia took to social media—

Page by page, she tore through Titobi's mother's obituary.

Mocked Titobi children.

Called them ugly.

Went live to degrade the dead and dishonor the living.

She weaponized grief.

She made cruelty a performance.

But God is still God.

And in 2022, when Letitia's two-year-old daughter was home with her

---

17-year-old son, someone knocked on the door.

Her son picked up his baby sister and opened it.

Standing there was someone sent to kill him.

And before they did, they gave him the courtesy of placing his sister

back inside.

She watched through the window as her brother was murdered.

Right in front of her eyes.

And Letitia?

She cried online.

Begged God for her son back.

Asked why this was happening to her–

As if she had forgotten the evil she had done to Titobi.

But scripture always reveals itself.

God always reminds us:

He is the true God.

The living God.

None of us is above His word.

And His word says:

"Vengeance is mine," thus saith the Lord.

Titobi kept that scripture close.

She didn't clap back.

She didn't go live.

She didn't drag Letitia through the mud.

Because God had already handled it.

In His way.

On His time.

With divine precision.

Titobi's grief had her tripping-looking for a bed warmer to take her mind

off the weight of becoming the matriarch, the head of her family.

She knew she was ready.

She just wanted to relax in someone's arms.

And that's when she met... something.

Alfred was his human name.

But good Lord-this was one of Satan's top-ranking evil soldiers.

He stood 5'4", straight out of Zambia, and bragged constantly about spending time on Devil's Street back home.

He boasted about his worldly knowledge, but what he truly worshipped

was alcohol.

He was an addict.

Addicted to alcohol.

Addicted to sin.

Addicted to fornication.

Addicted to everything ugly and unholy in this world.

And somehow, he landed right in Titobi's bed.

Right in her face.

Maybe this was the enemy-sending a distraction disguised as romance.

A counterfeit comfort.

A bed warmer wrapped in demonic intent.

He wasn't love.

He was a satanic minion sent to derail her destiny.

But Titobi always knew she was blessed.

Even in despair, she knew God had His hand on her.

She carried extreme favor.

And no matter what she faced, she would be okay.

This demon, though—he was different.

She'd dealt with demons before.

She'd had her covers warmed by confusion and chaos.

But Alfred's disguise was layered.

His greed, his trifling spirit—she could've seen it coming.

One night, in a drunken stupor, Alfred lost all control.

Titobi tried to calm him, but he ran down the street disturbing the

peace—

Yelling, exposing himself, acting out every demonic impulse imaginable.

And Titobi?

The good girl.

The God-fearing woman she was created to be—

She still entertained Alfred in his madness.

Not because she was weak.

But because she was trying to make sense of the storm.

Trying to find God in the chaos.

Trying to hold on to herself while grief tried to pull her under.

One day, while Titobi was trying to get Alfred back inside—he was outside disturbing the peace again—she saw something that confirmed everything her spirit had been whispering.

As he walked ahead of her, she saw two shadows.

One was Alfred.

The other was darker.

Not just in color, but in presence.

A shadow that didn't belong to the light.

She watched it follow him up the stairs.

And just as Alfred reached the door, she called out—

"Alfred, you are welcome in my house."

She said it loud.

Not for Alfred.

But for the demon trailing behind him.

She wanted that spirit to know:

I see you.

You are not welcome here.

And when the demon realized it had been acknowledged, it turned

around.

Alfred paused.

He looked confused.

Then he said, "I don't know why, but I'm not going in."

And there it was.

A smile.

On the shadow.

Grinning from the ground like it had won.

Titobi knew, right then and there, this wasn't just a man.

This was spiritual.

Not physical.

She had seen it with her own two eyes—

The demon guiding Alfred, controlling him, celebrating his chaos.

She should've left that day.

She should've never stayed another two years.

But she did.

And she learned.

She learned what it meant to be in the company of the enemy's people.

Because Titobi knows who she is.

She is chosen.

She is covered.

She cannot entertain the devil's children.

And Alfred?

Alfred was a spawn.

A vessel.

He and his mother—both looked like long-nosed witches, both carried the

same evil spirit.

Titobi should've known.

She should've run when she found out Alfred was having sexual relations with his own mother.

That was not love.

That was not ordained.

That was not God.

There's always some kind of peace in every storm.

During the passing of Titobi's mother, a quiet blessing emerged: she

reconnected with her cousin Ronald, whom she hadn't seen in over 20

years. Ronald was engaged to a lovely woman named Jolene—

affectionately called Cousin JoJo.

Titobi calls her Cousin JoJo because, married or not, she considers her

blood.

JoJo has a beautiful heart, a radiant spirit-another blessing sent by God into Titobi's life.

JoJo is from St. Martinville, Louisiana, a small parish just outside New Iberia.

And though she had certainly been warned to stay away from Titobi-fed the same ugly, mean-spirited rumors that circulate in whispers and side-eyes-Miss JoJo chose differently.

She followed her own heart.

Her own vision.

Her own understanding of God.

She gave Titobi a chance—not just to be known, but to be heard.

To share her side of the story.

To be seen beyond the tragedy.

Miss JoJo became a staple in Titobi's life.

She didn't judge her.

She wasn't concerned with what "they" said.

She got to know Titobi for herself—and in doing so, became the kind of

woman Titobi had needed for years.

Titobi has many older female cousins who could've guided her through

life—through heartbreak, womanhood, and survival.

But they didn't.

They hated her.

Despised her over trust fund rumors and the lies her family spread

around New Iberia.

None of them loved on her.

None of them stepped in to guide her.

Many of those cousins were on their second marriages, had lived through

divorce and hardship—but still chose silence over sisterhood.

Miss JoJo, though?

She's a fine, accomplished woman.

An A.K.A

A registered nurse.

A business owner.

A woman who's touched millions and understands culture beyond the hood.

Her wealth, her education, and her lived experience gave her discernment.

She wasn't easily swayed by gossip or bitterness.

She chose to know Titobi for herself.

And when she came into Titobi's life, she loved on her.

She allowed Titobi to love her back.

And just like that, Titobi had a new friendship-one that would carry her through the rest of her life.

Because when it came to Alfred, Titobi needed Miss JoJo more than she ever knew.

She didn't realize it at the time, but Miss JoJo would become her saving grace for what she was about to face on May 16, 2023.

May 16, 2023, he transformed into something unrecognizable.

He beat her—with a baseball bat.

Not a shove. Not an argument turned physical. A weapon.

He struck her within inches of her life. It wasn't passion. It was attempted murder. And in that moment, as her body collapsed and her breath became desperate, Titobi realized this wasn't just a man. He was a manifestation of every demon she'd ever survived.

And she did survive.

With broken ribs, bruised spirit, and bloodied memory—but a beating heart.

Because no matter how many times evil knocked, God was still guarding the door.

Chapter 8

The

Path

to Healing

After the brutal attack by Alfred, Titobi felt like she was on the verge of losing her mind. The physical pain was excruciating, but the emotional trauma was even more overwhelming. Alfred had not only beaten her almost to death but had also publicly humiliated her, leaving her to face the scorn and judgment of those around her. The betrayal and abandonment were a heavy burden on her heart, and Titobi struggled to find a way to cope.

In the aftermath of the attack, Titobi knew that she needed help to navigate the darkness that had enveloped her life. She began attending therapy sessions, seeking the guidance of a psychologist who could help her process the trauma and find a path to healing. The sessions were challenging, as Titobi had to confront the painful memories and emotions that she had tried to bury. But with each session, she began to unravel the layers of pain and slowly rebuild her sense of self.

Titobi's journey to recovery was not easy. She faced moments of despair and doubt, wondering if she would ever be able to move past the trauma. The public humiliation added to her struggles, as she felt the weight of judgment from those who knew about the attack. Titobi's faith became a crucial source of strength during this time. She leaned more towards her Latter-day Saints faith, finding solace in the teachings and the community that supported her.

Through prayer and reflection, Titobi found a sense of peace that had eluded her for so long. Her faith provided her with the resilience to face each day and the hope that she could overcome the challenges ahead.

The church became a sanctuary where she could find comfort and

guidance, and the support of the congregation helped her feel less alone.

Months of therapy and spiritual guidance began to show results. Titobi's

wounds, both physical and emotional, started to heal. She discovered a

newfound strength within herself, a determination to reclaim her life and

find happiness once again. The journey was long and arduous, but

Titobi's faith and perseverance carried her through.

As she continued to heal, Titobi began to open herself up to the

possibility of love once more. She knew that she deserved to be treated

with respect and kindness, and she was determined to find a partner

who would cherish her for who she was. Titobi's journey to recovery

was a testament to her resilience and the power of faith to guide her through even the darkest of times. That's it.

That's what Titobi was great at-healing.

She was masterful at picking herself up, carrying on, and refusing to stay

stuck.

So many things had tried to stop her in her tracks.

So many distractions, betrayals, and spiritual attacks meant to keep her

from walking in her calling.

But God had a purpose for her.

And Titobi kept moving toward it.

She's been blessed along the way-with a circle of supporters, friendships

that feel heaven-sent.

And she doesn't take a single one for granted.

Through her faith walk as a member of the Church of Jesus Christ of

Latter-day Saints, she found untold friendship and deep bonds with

younger Caucasian women who poured into her.

They reminded her of her worth.

They reassured her that it was more than okay to be Titobi.

That it was divine.

And without God, she wouldn't have survived everything she's been

through.

But with God—and these relationships—she did.

A lot of people don't realize how much love exists within the Mormon

faith.

They don't see the quiet acts of service, the daily affirmations, the ways this community helps people navigate life.

The love Titobi never received from her family or her hometown?

She received it from her sisters.

Her sisters showed up.

Let's be clear—*the brothers prayed,* and *the bishops waved,* but it was the sisters who plastered her door like it was Valentine's Day and finals week rolled into one.

Hearts, sticky notes, scriptures, affirmations—every morning felt like a spiritual pep rally.

They didn't just uplift her.

They reminded her she was loved, seen, and supported-loudly, creatively, and with enough glitter glue to make heaven smile.

Yes, people questioned her faith.

They questioned how a Black woman could be Mormon.

But Titobi never felt the need to explain her religion or justify the love God showed her through different paths.

She simply remained grateful-for her Mormon family and for every person who chose love over judgment.

In 2024, Titobi made her first pilgrimage to Salt Lake City, Utah, to attend one of her sisters' weddings-and it wasn't just any venue.

It was *the* temple.

The Salt Lake Temple stood like a carved hymn-majestic, sacred, and

impossibly still against the sky.

Walking up to it felt like stepping into a living testimony.

The spires reached toward heaven like they had something to say, and

the stone shimmered with generations of prayer.

Titobi didn't just witness a wedding-she witnessed legacy.

And in that moment, surrounded by love and light, she knew she was

exactly where God wanted her to be.

And without a doubt, they loved on her.

They welcomed her into their homes.

Their families had heard of her, embraced her, and treated her with the same warmth she'd always received when those girls visited her—

whether for lunch, prayer, or just presence.

Titobi will forever be grateful to God for her Mormon family.

Chapter 9

The

Therapist

Sessions

After the brutal attack by Alfred, Titobi felt like she was on the verge of losing her mind. The physical pain was excruciating, but the emotional trauma was even more overwhelming. Alfred had not only beaten her almost to death but had also publicly humiliated her, leaving her to face the scorn and judgment of those around her. The betrayal and abandonment were a heavy burden on her heart, and Titobi struggled to find a way to cope.

In the aftermath of the attack, Titobi knew that she needed help to navigate the darkness that had enveloped her life. She began attending therapy sessions, seeking the guidance of a psychologist who could help her process the trauma and find a path to healing. The sessions were challenging, as Titobi had to confront the painful memories and emotions that she had tried to bury. But with each session, she began to unravel

the layers of pain and slowly rebuild her sense of self.

Titobi's therapist, Dr. Williams, was a compassionate and skilled

professional who understood the complexities of trauma. Dr. Williams

created a safe and supportive environment where Titobi could express

her feelings without fear of judgment. The therapist sessions were a mix

of talk therapy, cognitive-behavioral techniques, and mindfulness

exercises, all designed to help Titobi regain control over her life.

During the sessions, Titobi explored the impact of Alfred's abuse on her

mental and emotional well-being. She discussed the feelings of shame,

guilt, and worthlessness that had plagued her since the attack. Dr.

Williams helped Titobi challenge these negative thoughts and replace

them with more empowering beliefs. The process was slow and often painful, but Titobi began to see glimpses of hope and resilience within herself.

One of the most significant breakthroughs came when Titobi confronted the public humiliation she had faced. Dr. Williams guided her through exercises that helped her reclaim her sense of dignity and self-worth. Titobi learned to separate her identity from the actions of others and to recognize her inherent value as a person. This shift in perspective was crucial in her journey to healing. In a powerful act of reclaiming her narrative, Titobi turned the tables on Alfred's attempts to publicly humiliate her. She took to her social media and bravely shared her own story, taking the power out of his hands. Alfred raced to her pages, attempting to challenge her facts and discredit her. However, his efforts only made him look foolish. In the end, he was forced to apologize, acknowledging the truth of her experiences and the strength she had shown in overcoming them. Titobi's courage in standing up for herself was a testament to the self-worth and confidence she had gained, thanks to her LDS family unwavering support.

As the months passed, Titobi's therapist sessions became a cornerstone of her recovery. She found solace in the structured environment and the consistent support of Dr. Williams. The sessions provided her with tools to manage her anxiety, cope with triggers, and build a more positive outlook on life. Titobi's faith also played a significant role in her healing process. She leaned more towards her LDS faith, finding comfort in the teachings and the community that supported her. As the months passed,

Titobi's therapy sessions became a cornerstone of her recovery.

Dr. Williams offered more than just clinical support—she created a space

where Titobi could unravel, rebuild, and rise.

The structured environment gave her tools to manage anxiety, navigate

triggers, and reframe her outlook on life.

But healing didn't just happen on the couch.

It happened in prayer.

In scripture.

In the quiet moments when her LDS faith reminded her she was never

alone.

She leaned into the teachings.

She leaned into the community.

And she leaned into the truth that had carried her through every storm:

God created therapists.

So we could have therapy *and* Jesus.

We don't have to pick one.

For Titobi, healing was never either/or.

It was both/and.

It was sacred and clinical.

It was spiritual and strategic.

It was divine design.

And with every session, every prayer, and every step forward, she knew—

She was walking in purpose.

She was walking in grace.

She was walking with God.

Chapter 10

The Power

of

Friendship

Titobi's journey to healing was marked by the support and guidance she received during her therapy sessions. These sessions became a cornerstone of her recovery, providing her with the tools to navigate the emotional turmoil and rebuild her sense of self. It was during one of these sessions that Titobi met Willisonia, a woman whose story was as heartbreaking as her own.

Willisonia had faced unimaginable betrayal and pain. Her husband had cheated on her and given her HIV, a devastating blow that shattered her trust and sense of security. The betrayal was compounded when Willisonia discovered her husband in bed with her nephew, a moment that left her feeling utterly broken and alone. Despite the immense pain, Willisonia was determined to heal and find a way forward.

Titobi and Willisonia quickly formed a bond, drawn together by their

shared experiences and the understanding that comes from facing life's

darkest moments. They supported each other through the ups and downs

of their therapy sessions, offering words of encouragement and a

shoulder to lean on. Willisonia's strength and resilience inspired Titobi,

and Titobi's unwavering faith provided Willisonia with a sense of hope.

As they navigated their healing journeys, Titobi helped Willisonia

reconnect with her faith. She shared her own experiences of finding

solace in prayer and the teachings of the church. Titobi encouraged

Willisonia to trust in God's plan and to believe that there was a path to

healing and redemption. Together, they attended church services and participated in faith-based activities, finding comfort in the community

and the support of the congregation.

Willisonia's journey was not without its challenges. The emotional scars

left by her husband's betrayal and the physical impact of HIV were

constant reminders of her pain. However, with Titobi's support and the

guidance of their therapist, Willisonia began to find a sense of peace. She

learned to forgive, to let go of the past, and to embrace the present with

gratitude.

Titobi's friendship with Willisonia became a source of strength for both

of them. They celebrated each other's victories, no matter how small, and

provided comfort during the difficult moments. Their bond was a testament to the power of friendship and the importance of having someone to lean on during times of hardship.

Through their shared journey, Titobi and Willisonia discovered the true meaning of resilience and faith. They learned that healing is a process, one that requires patience, support, and a belief in something greater. Together, they faced their challenges with courage and found a path to recovery that was filled with hope and love.

Chapter 11

The

Search

for

Love

After the court date with Alfred, Titobi knew without a shadow of a doubt that she had to leave him and begin a new chapter in her life. The court proceedings had been a painful reminder of the abuse and betrayal she had endured, but they also marked the beginning of her journey to reclaim her life and find happiness. With a renewed sense of determination, Titobi decided to explore the world of dating, hoping to find a partner who would treat her with the respect and love she deserved.

Titobi's dating life was a whirlwind of experiences. She met a variety of men, each with their own unique qualities and backgrounds. Titobi was—and still is—a gorgeous woman. Not the kind of gorgeous that fades under fluorescent lights, but the kind that holds court in every room she enters. Her beauty has always been more than skin deep: it's radiant,

spiritual, ancestral, and anchored in resilience. And because of it, she

drew attention from every direction—pastors with polished sermons and

bad intentions, clowns in disguise with oversized egos and undersized

integrity.

She didn't just date a few bad apples. She had loved—and survived—every

demon in hell's address book. And yet, she emerged glowing.

Now, fully aware of her divine worth, her dating pool looks different. Her

taste evolved. Her standards ascended. It's no longer enough to be

charming or fine—she seeks alignment. Purpose. Peace. Because being

loved isn't enough if it comes without honor. And no man will ever again sit at her table and eat from the plate God prepared—if he didn't help set it.

Among them were a few millionaires who dazzled her with their wealth and charm. One of these men was a real estate owner from Nigeria who took her out on a very expensive date. The evening was filled with luxury and excitement, but when he tried to sleep with her on the first date, Titobi knew that this relationship was not meant to be. She declined his advances, realizing that she was looking for something deeper and more meaningful.

Despite the setbacks, Titobi remained hopeful and continued to meet men online. She encountered a mix of personalities, some genuine and others less so. The process was often frustrating, but Titobi's faith and resilience kept her going. She knew that God had a plan for her, and she

trusted that the right person would come into her life at the right time.

Over the years, Titobi's beauty had drawn in every kind of man-pastors

with wandering eyes, clowns in love with the idea of her, manipulators

dressed in charm, and charmers cloaked in manipulation. She had

entertained spiritual leaders, street philosophers, and everything in

between. But after loving and surviving every demon in hell's directory,

she finally realized: being desired wasn't the same as being deserving.

And being chosen wasn't the same as being cherished.

Now she was selective. Guarded, but not bitter. Spiritually armed and

emotionally unavailable to chaos.

So, when Timothy stepped into the room, he caught her attention-not by

rehearsed compliments or recycled greetings, but with six words:

"Hey, I'm a Libra-like you."

He didn't say "Hey beautiful." She'd heard that a million times. His

opening line was subtle, intentional, and sacred. It pierced straight into

her zodiac-loving heart. As a proud libra who deeply admired the Libra

energy, she felt seen. When the male Libra met the female Libra, it

wasn't just romance-it was divine choreography. Their connection echoed

through the heavens like a Toni Braxton ballad, aching and elegant,

wrapped in velvet and testimony. It was the kind of love that didn't need

explanation, only recognition. Like Usher's confessions, it was smooth,

spiritual, and soul-baring.

They didn't just see each other—they *mirrored* each other. Two scales, perfectly balanced. Two hearts, ruled by Venus, speaking in rhythm and reverence. Their bond felt like something Cardi B would shout from a rooftop—bold, unapologetic, and blessed.

And in that moment, Titobi remembered the Libra legends who had walked this path before her. Will Smith, who turned reinvention into ritual. Lil Wayne, who tattooed the scales on his skin like scripture. T.I., who didn't just claim the sign—he *declared* it, naming an entire album after the legacy.

Even Kim Kardashian, with her Libra-born diplomacy and divine disruption, reminded Titobi that beauty and justice could coexist. That glam could be gospel. That balance could be a brand.

This wasn't just love.

This was spiritual symmetry.

This was God whispering, "Yes."

Timothy? That man was fine honey, with his soul identical to her's together they were everything a spirit lead couple should be.

She was already 99% divine-legacy-rooted, rhythmically aligned, dipped in testimony and wrapped in satin wit. But Timothy? Timothy was that final 1% that sent her over the top, through the clouds, and straight into the throne room of excess. He didn't walk into her life-he *glided*, like a Libra prince fresh out of a dream curated by Beyoncé and approved by God Himself. Beautiful? Absolutely. Handsome? Offensively so. Sexy? In a way that made mirrors blush and aunties clutch their pearls. His smile had diplomatic immunity. His walk had soundtrack energy. And when he spoke, even her ancestors leaned in. He wasn't just fine-he was spiritually *fined,* like heaven had charged extra for the audacity. Titobi didn't fall in love.

She *levitated.*

He was smooth. Soft-spoken, articulate, unbothered. Like Denzel had stepped off the screen and into her inbox. He didn't rush. Didn't brag. Just offered clarity wrapped in calm.

With her-full Southern Louisiana accent blazing-told him she wasn't interested in settling down, wasn't trying to date anyone from Africa, and was living fully in her soft-life glow, Timothy smiled. Not a smug smile. But a patient one.

She explained that A African man had betrayed her. That she wasn't

ready. That her body was new, her spirit was rising, and the millionaires

in her face were giving her luxury and laughter. She told Timothy: "We

can be friends. But it'll never be more than that."

Timothy laughed gently, then paused.

And then, with the same calm conviction that made her stop scrolling

and start listening, he replied:

"God has sent me to be your husband. I've come to claim you as my

wife."

Secretly a prince, Timothy, was unlike anyone she had met before. He

was kind, respectful, and had a deep sense of empathy. Timothy

understood the pain Titobi had endured and offered her a safe space to heal. Their conversations were filled with laughter, shared dreams, and a sense of connection that Titobi had longed for.

Timothy's background as a prince added an element of intrigue to their relationship. He was well-educated, cultured, and had a strong sense of duty to his family and community. Despite his royal status, Timothy was humble and down-to-earth, qualities that endeared him to Titobi. Their relationship blossomed, and Titobi felt a sense of peace and stability that she had not experienced ever before.

As they spent more time together, Titobi and Timothy discovered that they shared many values and aspirations. They supported each other through life's challenges and celebrated each other's successes. Titobi's journey to Timothy wasn't just a testament to resilience-it was a spiritual receipt stamped "Paid in Full." After seasons of silence,

heartbreak, and unanswered prayers, her heart had finally found a home.

Not just any home-a sanctuary. And Timothy? He wasn't just a man. He

was an angel in sneakers, hand-delivered from God with a wink and a

whisper: *"I saw your tears. Here's double for your trouble."*

His presence felt like divine acknowledgment. Like heaven had been

watching the whole time, taking notes, and waiting for the perfect

moment to send her a gift wrapped in grace and dipped in cologne. With

Timothy, she didn't just feel loved-she felt *seen.* Every ache, every

prayer, every lonely night had led to this: a love so intentional, it could

only be heaven-sent.

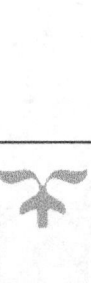

Chapter 12

Love Found

Titobi's journey had been one of transformation and self-discovery. As she looked back on the chapters of her life, she realized how far she had come. The pain and abuse she had endured were now memories that fueled her strength and resilience. Gabriel's love had been a catalyst for her growth, but it was her own determination that had carried her forward.

In this new chapter of her life, Titobi was ready to embrace the future with open arms. She had learned to love herself, to see her own worth, and to stand tall with confidence. The lessons she had learned from life and the experiences she had gone through had shaped her into the strong, independent woman she had become.

As she moved forward, Titobi knew that her journey was far from over.

There would be new challenges to face, new lessons to learn, and new

memories to create. But she was ready for whatever the future held,

knowing that she had the strength and resilience to overcome anything

that came her way.

And so, with a heart full of hope and a spirit unbroken, Titobi stepped

into the next chapter of her life, ready to embrace the future and all the

possibilities it held.

Timothy was a handsome prince, standing tall with a regal presence that

commanded attention. Despite his royal status, Timothy came from a

humble background. He was the heir to a Nigerian clothing brand that

had made close to a billion dollars in revenue in 2023. However,

Timothy's upbringing had instilled in him values of humility and

compassion. He was not defined by his wealth or title, but by his

character and the way he treated others.

Timothy was in search of a beautiful duchess who could sit beside him

and help him fulfill his duties as the first heir to the throne. He wanted

a partner who shared his values and aspirations, someone who could

support him in his journey and stand by his side through life's

challenges. Titobi's strength, resilience, and unwavering faith made her

the perfect match for Timothy. Along with her Education in marketing in

management she studied at Texas Southern University, gave her the

necessary education that would be needed to help Timothy take over the

family business in his time.

Timothy was shy and reserved, keeping his royal status a secret until he

was sure that she was his rib. He wanted to ensure that his future

partner loved him for who he was, not for his title or wealth. This

humility and sincerity endeared him to Titobi even more. As they spent

more time together, Titobi and Timothy discovered that they shared many

values and aspirations. They supported each other through life's

challenges and celebrated each other's successes. Titobi's journey to

finding Timothy was a testament to her resilience and the power of faith

to guide her through even the darkest of times.

Chapter 13

A

New

Beginning

Timothy's love for Titobi was unwavering, and he was determined to help her start a new chapter in her life. He knew that she needed to leave her past behind and embrace a future filled with hope and happiness. Using his resources, Timothy set out to help Titobi obtain a passport and make the necessary arrangements for her to join him in Nigeria.

Timothy's staff worked tirelessly to ensure that everything was in place. They coordinated with the authorities, expedited the paperwork, and provided Titobi with all the support she needed. The process was smooth and efficient, thanks to Timothy's influence and the dedication of his team.

As the day of departure approached, Titobi to travel across the world to her prince. Titobi felt a mix of excitement and nervousness. She was leaving behind the pain and trauma of her past and stepping into a new world filled with possibilities. Timothy's unwavering support and love gave her the strength to take this bold step.

Timothy's unwavering support gave her the strength to begin again.

After surviving heartbreak, betrayal, abandonment, and physical assault, Titobi was finally stepping into a season that felt divine. Timothy's love didn't just offer comfort—it offered clarity. It gave her permission to dream out loud. To board a plane alone. To let herself be loved without strings or suffering.

She booked the trip.

Destination: Africa.

First stop: London.

It would be her first time setting foot in another country. And of course,

she did it with flair. She touched down at Heathrow with a 24-hour

layover and a spirit of adventure that felt like prophecy fulfilled.

From the moment she saw the Louis Vuitton and Gucci boutiques in the

terminal, she knew: this layover was about to be legendary. Because this

time, she wasn't window-shopping with longings she was living,

breathing, and spending with freedom.

Timothy had linked his debit card to her Apple Pay.

Just like that, she had access to money that didn't come with shame,

strings, or self-sacrifice. After a lifetime of stretching pennies and sacrificing joy for survival, she could finally buy what she wanted—

without guilt.

Because Titobi had always been somebody's mother.

Since 14.

She had fed, clothed, protected, and nurtured her children with love, grit, and no help. The fathers, especially baby daddy number three, had made financial warfare their weapon of choice. Instead of support, he offered silence. Instead of parenting, he offered pressure. And he owed her—over $70,000 in unpaid child support.

But she didn't wait. Didn't chase. She kept mothering anyway.

Even though she had once been labeled a "trust fund baby," her mother had already drained those accounts before she came of age. Titobi was rich in spirit, but poor on paper. She lived structured, disciplined, resourceful-because she had to. She begged no man for anything and wore struggle like satin when necessary.

Still, they used finances as a form of punishment. They knew that by starving her purse, they could try to starve her power.

But Timothy had disarmed that curse.

And in that London airport, shopping on her own, breathing with ease, holding God's grace in one hand and a Chanel bag in the other-Titobi cried.

Not from grief.

Not from regret.

From realization.

She was living a life she once feared she'd never touch.

She was alone but loved.

She was abroad but anchored.

She was broken once, but now free.

In that moment, she thanked God aloud.

In that moment, she praised like royalty.

In that moment, she remembered who she was:

A survivor.

A mother.

A miracle.

And for 24 hours, London looked a little brighter. Because for 24 hours,

she was walking like the Duchess of Sussex-with her crown made of

testimony and her throne built of trust.

Chapter 14

Back to the

Crown

Lagos, Love,

and Legacy

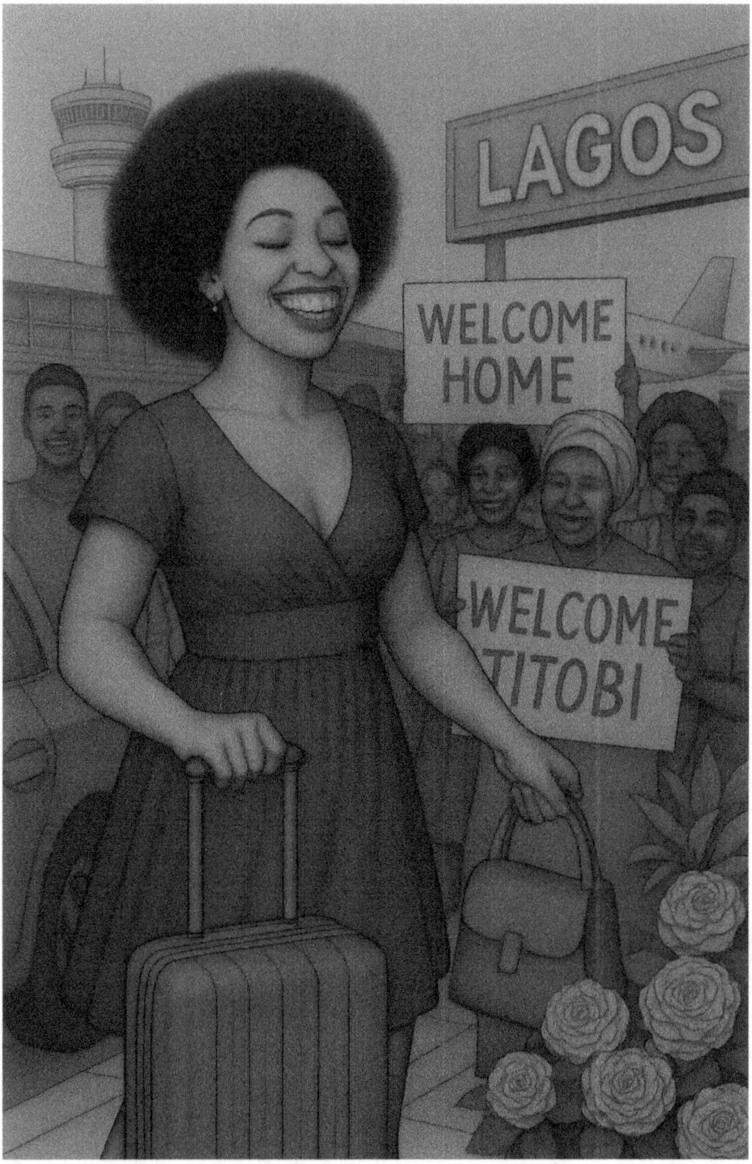
LAGOS
WELCOME
HOME
WELCOME
TITOBI

Titobi's journey to Nigeria was filled with anticipation and hope. She

knew that she was embarking on a new adventure, one that would

change her life forever. As the plane touched down in Lagos, Titobi's

heart raced with excitement. She was about to meet Timothy, the man

who had captured her heart and offered her a future filled with love and

happiness.

Timothy's staff had arranged for a luxurious car to pick Titobi up from

the airport. The drive through the bustling streets of Lagos was a

sensory overload, with vibrant colors, lively music, and the rich aroma of

local cuisine filling the air. Titobi felt a deep sense of connection to the

land, knowing that this was where her new life would begin. Titobi had

always dreamed of returning to the motherland. To walk barefoot on the ground, where her roots had derived history was stolen and her culture was planted. And so, with a heart full of hope and a spirit unbroken, Titobi stepped into the next chapter of her life, ready to embrace the future and all the possibilities it held.

Her destination? Lagos, Nigeria.

Her reason? Love—and legacy.

This wasn't just a passport stamp. It was spiritual migration. It was healing handed to her in Yoruba rhythm and West African air.

The moment her plane descended, and the Lagos skyline emerged, her breath shifted.

Each inhale felt ancestral.

Each exhale felt like coming home.

Every African American who can-must find their way to Africa.

There's no metaphor strong enough.

You breathe differently.

You stand differently.

You belong differently.

Africa doesn't just receive you, it remembers you.

It's a spiritual experience that defies language. The dust feels familiar.

The music feels inherited. The rhythm feels like your grandmother's

prayer. The connection is instant-vibrational.

And when Titobi stepped into Lagos, she felt it deeply. Not just because Timothy was there waiting like a prince with palm wine and patience, but because the land itself acknowledged her arrival.

And she was still on a high remembering how she navigated the airport, eyes wide, spirit soaring, she passed Louis Vuitton and Gucci stores with a sparkle in her eye. Not because she needed labels-but because she could now choose. Timothy had linked his debit card to her Apple Pay. For the first time in her life, she was able to spend with joy and freedom-on herself.

And for once, she didn't feel guilt. She didn't feel burden. She felt worthy.

Not just love but luxury.

Not just of survival—but of abundance.

This was different.

She had lived under the weight of financial oppression. Baby Daddy #3

owed her over $70,000 in unpaid child support and never offered help.

He punished her by withholding what belonged to their child, leaving her

to stretch pennies and hope. But now?

Now, she had access.

Now, she had choices.

Now, she had peace.

In London, during a 24-hour layover, she shopped. She smiled. She

praised.

By the time she touched Nigerian soil, she had transitioned from survivor to sacred traveler.

Timothy welcomed her like a king ready to honor his queen-not with flashy gestures, but with spiritual intention.

And Lagos welcomed her like a daughter returned home.

It was loud. Vibrant. Beautiful.

The food. The fabrics. The language.

The breath. Oh, the breath.

Africa taught her how to inhale legacy.

And every reader of her story-every woman, every man, every Black child with a dream-should feel this for themselves.

Go home.

Touch the land.

Let Africa remind you who you are.

Titobi had always dreamed of returning to the motherland. To walk

barefoot on the ground, where her roots had derived history was stolen

and her culture was planted.

As the car approached Timothy's estate, Titobi's excitement grew. The

grand entrance was adorned with elegant decorations, and the lush

greenery created a serene and welcoming atmosphere. The car came to a

stop, and Titobi stepped out, her heart pounding with anticipation.

Timothy stood at the entrance, waiting for her. He was dressed in

traditional Nigerian attire, his regal presence commanding attention. As

their eyes locked, a wave of emotion washed over both of them. The

connection they had felt through their conversations was now tangible,

and the love they shared was undeniable.

Timothy walked towards Titobi, his eyes filled with warmth and affection.

The world seemed to fade away as they moved closer to each other.

When they finally stood face to face, the air was charged with electricity.

Without a word, Timothy gently cupped Titobi's face in his hands and

leaned in, their lips meeting in a tender and passionate kiss.

The kiss was a moment of pure magic, a culmination of their journey and

the beginning of their future together. It was filled with love, hope, and the promise of a life filled with happiness. As they pulled away, Timothy

whispered,

"Welcome home, my Beautiful Duchess." Titobi was startled by

everything. As the gates of the family compound opened, Titobi felt her

breath catch.

She was greeted by a massive staff, a sea of smiling faces, and the visual

poetry of thousands of roses, their petals cascading like welcome

prayers. The air was warm with celebration. Timothy's extended family

stood waiting-not with hesitation, but with open arms. Laughter and

reverence wove through the crowd like music.

His father, tall and regal, stood near the entrance, surrounded by multiple

wives-the fulfillment of traditions born from generations of Yoruba

heritage. In that moment, Titobi didn't judge. She understood the rhythm

of this life, the layers of legacy and the spiritual design behind familial

expansion. Here, wives were respected. Children were cradled in

collective love. Legacy mattered. Timothy's mother was the first wife—the

traditional wife. Hardworking, graceful, and undeniably beautiful. It was

easy to see where Timothy got his striking features: the bone structure,

the quiet elegance, and that unforgettable smile. His smile was hers. A

radiant inheritance.

She wasn't just admired—she was legendary. In her village, people still

told the story of how, at just 14 years old, she faced down a wild lion

and killed it with her bare hands. That kind of strength wasn't just

physical—it was spiritual, ancestral, divine. And Titobi felt it instantly. She saw herself in that woman. Two women, cut from the same cloth:

strong, loving, protective, and deeply rooted in purpose.

Timothy's mother carried a quiet power. She didn't need to raise her

voice to command respect. Her strength was steady, her silence sacred.

Timothy had inherited that too-his stillness, his depth, his ability to hold

space without needing to fill it with noise.

And when Titobi stood beside him, their spiritual gifts collided like

thunder. The kind of energy that could knock someone to the floor-not

from fear, but from reverence. Together, they were a force. A divine

pairing. Proof that God doesn't just match hearts-He matches legacies.

And for Titobi, who had long considered herself a self-proclaimed

orphan-not by death, but by emotional abandonment-it felt holy.

She had walked away from the cruelty of her mother's side in Louisiana,

choosing solitude over mistreatment. But here, in the warmth of this

compound, she was enveloped by belonging.

This wasn't just Timothy's family. It was now hers.

A woven tapestry of aunties and brothers, cooks and cousins, nannies

and nieces. It was the family God had prepared, when Louisiana slammed

its doors and tried to convince her she'd never be enough.

She didn't just feel welcome, she felt chosen.

And standing beside Timothy, roses at her feet and legacy blooming around her, Titobi knew this was another divine promise fulfilled.

Timothy had kept the secret of his royal heritage hidden for almost a year, never once mentioning that he was a prince. "Titobi's heart swelled with joy. Titobi realized that God's lifelong promises to her were finally starting to manifest."

She knew that she had found her soulmate, the person who would stand by her side through all of life's challenges. Together, they walked hand in hand into the estate, ready to embrace their new life and the love that had brought them together.

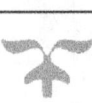

Chapter 14.5

A

Night

Of

Romance

As Titobi and Timothy arrived at the estate, the grandeur of the compound took her breath away. The entrance was adorned with elegant decorations, and the lush greenery created a serene and welcoming atmosphere. The estate was a testament to Timothy's royal heritage, yet it exuded warmth and intimacy that made Titobi feel at home.

Timothy led Titobi through the beautifully landscaped gardens, their path illuminated by soft, twinkling lights. The air was filled with the fragrance of blooming flowers, and the gentle sound of a nearby fountain added to the enchantment of the evening. Titobi's heart raced with anticipation, knowing that this night would be one to remember.

As they entered the estate, Timothy guided Titobi to a private room that had been meticulously prepared for their romantic evening. The room was filled with the soft glow of candlelight, casting a warm and inviting ambiance. The flickering flames danced in harmony with the soothing jazz music that played in the background, creating an atmosphere of pure romance.

Timothy's attention to detail was evident in every aspect of the room. Decorated in purple and gold royal fixings. The bed was adorned with luxurious silk sheets, and the air was infused with the calming scent of essential oils. Titobi felt a sense of peace and tranquility wash over her as she took in the beauty of the setting.

With His gentle, breathtaking, heart-pausing smile., Timothy approached Titobi and began to Passionately kiss her while sliding down the straps to her sexy satin black dress. While slowly kissing her with the intentions

of undressing her slowly and smoothly.

His touch was tender and respectful, making her feel cherished and

adored. As he removed her clothing, Timothy's eyes never left hers,

conveying a deep sense of love and admiration.

Once Titobi was comfortably undressed, he complimented every inch of

her birthday suit. Expressing how beautiful God had made every inch of

her.

He carefully helped Titobi onto the table, where he had laid a bed of

fresh Juliet roses and saffron flowers. The scent of the Safron's filled

the room with a captivating aroma of romance. Both Titobi and Timothy

were deeply drawn to each other, but they had agreed not to indulge in their feelings until they became husband and wife. They shared a beautiful, sensual, and unforgettable night together."

Timothy began to give her a body massage with warm ginger and black seed oil. His hands moved with skill and care, easing the tension in her muscles and soothing her mind. The warmth of the oil and the gentle pressure from his soft strong hands put her into a calming nap. Timothy, realizing she had now fallen asleep, wrapped his warm, naked body over hers as if he were a warm human quilt and they slept the night away in sensual bliss.

Chapter 15

The Proposal

Timothy's love for Titobi was unwavering, and he wanted to show her just how much she meant to him. He planned a grand and lavish proposal that would be a testament to his deep affection and commitment. The proposal took place on the south lawn of the family's estate, surrounded by the natural beauty of Nigeria.

Timothy chose a picturesque spot overlooking the serene waters of the compound's lake, with lush greenery and vibrant flowers creating a breathtaking backdrop. The setting was adorned with elegant decorations, including twinkling fairy lights, delicate floral arrangements, and luxurious royal drapery. The atmosphere was magical, filled with an air of romance and anticipation.

As the sun began to set, casting a warm golden glow over the landscape, Timothy led Titobi to the center of the beautifully decorated area. A soft melody played in the background, by the staffed violinist, adding to the enchantment of the moment. Timothy's heart raced with excitement and love as he prepared to ask the most important question of his life.

With a gentle smile, Timothy got down on one knee and presented Titobi with an engagement ring. He had a customized 75-carat pink and purple raw crystal-clear diamond ring made just for her.

The ring was a symbol of his love and commitment, carefully chosen to reflect the depth of his feelings. The diamonds sparkled in the fading light, capturing the essence of their journey together.

Timothy's words were heartfelt and sincere. He spoke of the incredible bond they shared, the challenges they had overcame, and the dreams they had for the future. His voice was filled with emotion as he expressed his desire to spend the rest of his life with Titobi, to cherish and support her through every moment.

He was still on one knee, eyes locked on hers, smiling with that quiet confidence she knew so well. He didn't speak right away. Instead, he reached for his hat—the one she'd teased him about in nearly every late-night call—and gently placed it at her feet.

Titobi, ever the comedian and vessel of wisdom, had joked for months:

"You better drop that hat when you propose, sir. I need drama and divinity." And now, here it was. Drama. Divinity. Delivered.

Timothy, the brilliant engineer with a wit that could rival her own, gave

her a moment to absorb it. He waited for her smile—the one that always

made his chest feel like revival—and when it came, he burst into laughter.

She joined him, their joy echoing like a private praise break.

Then he spoke.

"Titobi... I will always protect and cover you.

I will always go to God on your behalf.

I want to label you with my father's name,

and cover you with the Father's blood.

Just as my father covered my mother—with his name and the blood—I ask

you to let me do the same.

Please... allow me to cover you."

It wasn't just a proposal. It was a covenant. A spiritual alignment. A generational vow. And in that moment, with the hat at her feet and heaven leaning in, Titobi knew: this wasn't just love. This was legacy.

Titobi's eyes filled with tears of joy as she listened to Timothy's heartfelt proposal. The love and sincerity in his words touched her deeply, and she knew that this was the moment she had been waiting for. With a radiant smile, she accepted Timothy's proposal, knowing that their future together would be filled with love, happiness, and endless possibilities.

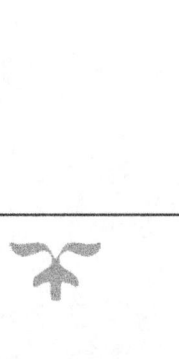

Chapter 16

The

Meaning

of

Titobi

Now that they were engaged and planning their wedding, they had fun exchanging and teaching each other about their cultural backgrounds. Titobi, being from Louisiana, and Timothy, being from Nigeria, were always shocked by the similarities in their backgrounds.

As they delved deeper into each other's cultures, they discovered many shared values and traditions. Both Louisiana and Nigerian cultures placed a strong emphasis on family, with gatherings and celebrations being important aspects of life. Their culinary traditions were rich and flavorful, with spicy dishes that reminded them of home. Music and dance played significant roles in both cultures, and they found joy in sharing their favorite songs and dances with each other.

Religious practices were also a common thread, with both cultures having

a significant presence of Christianity. They attended church together,

finding comfort in their shared faith. Storytelling traditions brought

them closer, as they shared tales passed down through generations,

preserving their history and folklore.

Festivals and celebrations were vibrant and colorful in both cultures.

Titobi and Timothy looked forward to experiencing each other's festivals,

from Mardi Gras in Louisiana to the Eyo Festival in Lagos. These

similarities created a strong bond between them, making their journey

together even more enriching and meaningful.

As they continued to plan their wedding, they knew that their love and

shared cultural heritage would be the foundation of their future together.

They were excited to build a life filled with love, respect, and understanding, celebrating the beautiful blend of their backgrounds. After the proposal, Timothy asked Titobi a question that had been on his mind for a long time. "Titobi, do you know what your name means in Yoruba?" he asked, his eyes filled with love and curiosity.

Titobi shook her head, "No, Timothy, I don't."

Timothy smiled and took her hand, "It means 'Big.' You are destined for greatness, Titobi. Your name reflects your strength, resilience, and the incredible journey you have been on. You are my beautiful Duchess, and together, we will build a future filled with love and happiness."

After Titobi discovered the meaning of her name, she stood in awe. It all made sense now. *Titobi* wasn't just a name-it was a revelation. A mirror.

A rhythm. It was everything her Heavenly Father had ever been in her life: big, bold, beautiful, and unwavering.

God had shown up in every inch of her experience. In the laughter, in the loss. In the silence, and in the sound. *Titobi* was in her. *Titobi* was in Timothy. *Titobi* was in everyone. Because God is big. God is beautiful. God is faithful, forgiving, and absolutely amazing.

And being the artist she is, her creativity caught fire. She ran out of the compound barefoot, racing down the street like a child chasing a kite. Timothy chased after her, laughing, "Girl, you're American-remember who your president is!" She hollered back, "I'm Nigerian today!" already on her iPhone Pro Max, searching for Lagos studios.

She found one. And she was ready to walk there if she had to.

The Spirit had always spoken to her. Loud. Clear. Unapologetic. At six

years old, she sat on the porch with her mother and grandmother and

said, "There's about to be a fire." They laughed. Minutes later, the back

of the house on Edna Street was in flames.

At eight, she told her mother, "I'm sorry." Her mother asked, "For what,

honey?" Titobi replied, "Today's the day Grandma dies." And when she

came home from school, her grandmother was gone.

She could always see death. Hear the Spirit. Feel the shift.

When Aunt Pat passed in 2004, it was the first time she saw the Spirit

with her bare eyes—comforting her, whispering, *I will never leave you.*

So when the Spirit spoke now, she knew to listen. She grabbed her

phone, opened Notes, and started writing every word. The rhythm was

African. The pulse was divine. She felt the urge to dance like David danced.

She recited lyrics to Timothy as he called the staff to prep the studio. He didn't think she was crazy. Everything about her mirrored him—and he loved it.

They arrived at a dark, tucked-away studio in the back of Ikeja. Titobi burst in like a fireball, singing:

"Anything and everything I ask of You,

You will do it times two!"

Her praise was loud. Her joy contagious. The producer lit up, sat at his keyboard, and started crafting the beat to match her spirit. The session was electric. Timothy called the staff to cover the bill and prep for

departure.

On the ride back to the compound, joy filled the air. Timothy teased her

lyrics—"You better days, better days!"—and then, as a pastor and a witness,

he turned to her and said:

"I tell you the truth.

No servant is greater than his master,

Nor is a messenger greater than the one who sent him.

But God gives us a command:

Love each other as He has loved us.

He is Titobi.

And Titobi is in all of us.

Titobi is you."

TITOBI

DEDICATION:

To my mother, Sheryl Ann Wilfred (April 7, 1950 –
January 9, 2020),

Momma, I hope you knew how deeply I loved you.
The enemy placed many obstacles in the middle of
our relationships some battles we won, and others we
lost. But through it all, you, Patricia Wilfred Dugas,
and Antionette Wilfred Chachere raised me to be a
God-fearing Southern belle. Every day, I honor every
inch of the woman you shaped me to be.

To my father, JHJ:

who left this earth when I was just two years old. I
don't remember you—but I thank you for my voice,
my unwavering faith, and this dominant, red Texas
blood flowing through me. I'm doing everything I can
with it.

Florita, Mildred, Bertha, and Velma:

I know my roots. I come from a line of strong, Indian Creole women, and I honor that legacy within myself every single day.

To my cousin-brother Corey Chachere:

In December of 2024, you were struck by a car and left for dead. I remember going to the hospital and personally asking God to do me a favor. I had never in my life been bold enough to ask God for a favor, but on that day, I knew I needed Him to move. I begged God to save your life and bring you to Him so you could live more abundantly— above all you can ask or think—with our Lord and Savior Jesus Christ leading the way.

You've always been a very good big brother to me. Sure, we've had our obstacles, especially given the contrast in our backgrounds—me, the so-called trust fund baby—but I'm glad you are still here. I honor where God has taken us and where He is taking us. I see a strength in you that I've never seen before.

The day you went into surgery, I was scared and prayed hard. I remembered you telling me to stop all that praying, and how you looked at the surgery staff and said, "Let's rock." That line will forever be embedded in my memory as a symbol of your courage—and a reminder of the strength I come from.

I will always honor the times you stood by me the best you could, and I want you to know I love you, big brother cousin.

To Dana, a.k.a. Big Gerald's wife:

You will always be my sister. I love you deeply. The spirit sent you at the exact moment I needed truth, and you spoke every word of Habakkuk 2:2 with divine clarity. I followed your wisdom. I wrote the vision. I made it plain. This book, this legacy, this healing—it began with your healing voice.

To my cousin Josephine: (My Jo-Jo)

Thank you for supporting me and helping me grow into a better woman. You stood by me in spite of the rumors and the lies. You could've turned your back, but you didn't. I will always love you for that.

To my cousin Roy:

Every morning, you wake up and send me encouraging scriptures and prayers. That's what a big brother and big cousin should do. I love you for that. I love our relationship for that. Thank you, cousin.

To my cousin Javarick:

Yes, I'm going to go ahead and call you cousin. You keep me grounded, and you already know—we got to talk mad X about this book!

To my children:

I have never, will never, and do not aspire to be perfect. But believe this: our Heavenly Father loves each of you deeply, without demanding perfection.

To Willie J.

We met at Texas Southern, School of Communications— graduation class of (don't worry, I won't tell your business this time).

You've always pushed me to do more, be more, and show up fully—even when we're just sitting around eating like family. I cook, you grill, and somehow those barbecue sausages keep selling themselves.

Sunny Side never owed me anything, but it gave me everything.
And Cloverland raised a good man—I see that. Always have.

Thank you for being a real one in a world that forgets how.

To my baby boy, Ty Ty:

My fifth-born child, my third son, you are so very special to me—and even more so to God. Always know that. Always remember that. You've had such a hard life, yet you are such a blessed and extraordinary child. You're amazing, and you're going to take the world by storm. I apologize for the attacks on your life from your siblings. I apologize for the lack of love they've shown you. I apologize for your absent father. I'm sorry for the pain that rests heavy on your little heart. Mama wishes so desperately that I could fix it all. But I know who holds all the answers, and if you always put your faith and trust in God, you will never be forsaken.

God is not a respecter of man—God is a respecter of favor. And you have divine favor over your life. God will never leave you nor forsake you, son, not even until the end of time. Trust your Bible. Trust the scriptures. Trust the promises God has made to you. Always let God live in your heart—no matter how deeply the world hurts or attacks you.

As long as you depend on God, you will be okay. You will always be okay. Never stop believing. Never stop trusting. God is amazing. He is awesome. And He will hold you— even when no one else does.

Always, always, always—Mama is praying, and God is with you.

To my one and only sibling,

<u>Big Boss Man Wilfred:</u>

I am so proud of you

Texas Southern University's

School of Business Graduate

You are the beat of my heart. The world knows that.

I apologize to you—for having to walk through this life as my brother.

I apologize for the family who never gave you a chance because they couldn't see past their hatred for me.

They betrayed you, attacked you, neglected you—all because you are my sibling.

They never gave you room to be loved for who you are. And for that, I publicly apologize.

I love you, brother. I love you deeply.

And I'm going to stick by you—the best I can—until the wheels fall off.

I thank God for you.

I thank God for your strength.

I thank God that

I am never alone because

have you.

To my amazing husband:

Sir, you already know.

you are the crème de la crème!

The icing on my cake.

The blessing that God, tucked away until I was
spiritually ready to receive you.

You are all that—and a bag of chips.

No words could ever fully explain to this world the
value you've restored in me.

You are everything a king should be!!! Everything God
created a king to be!

You are everything that the queen in me needs to
breathe.

Every breath I take—you're in it.

You are a living artwork.

A beautiful African king.

A gift from God Himself.

And I am so grateful.

I am so thankful.

I love you, my king!

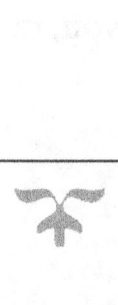

TITOBI'S INSPIRATIONAL

LOVE

JOURNAL

Written By: Invigorating Duchess

1 CORINTHIANS 13

"Love is patient, love is kind..."

When bruised by time and trials past,

Love held my hand, firm and steadfast.

Not loud or proud, it chose the slow-

To heal in silence, let peace grow.

-

JOHN 3:16

"For God so loved the world..."

A love that gave without demand,

Stretched wide its arms across the land.

No throne too high, no soul too lost,

He paid the price-He bore the cost.

-

---

1 JOHN 4:7-8

"Beloved, let us love one another..."

Love isn't merely sweet or light,

It's strength in pain; it's truth in fight.

The breath of God within our chest—

To love is life; to love is blessed.

-

ROMANS 5:8

"While we were still sinners, Christ died for us."

I wore my wounds like armor tight,

Ashamed to stand beneath His light.

Yet even then-through sin, through strife-

He claimed me first and gave me life.

-

1 PETER 4:8

"Above all, love each other deeply..."

Love covers shame and scars that bleed,

It answers prayer and meets the need.

A depth not seen but deeply felt–

In arms of grace, I rose, I knelt.

www.ingramcontent.com/pod-product-compliance
Lightning Source LLC
Chambersburg PA
CBHW050340030726
47503CB00008B/2536